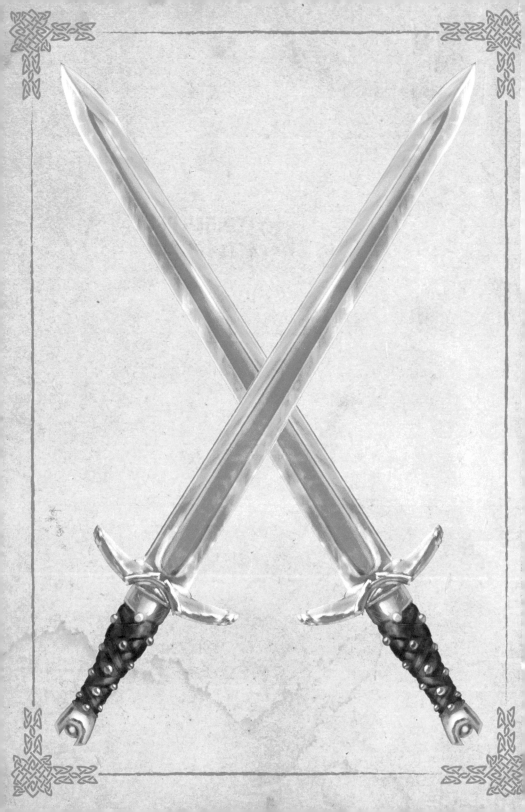

Escape the Underdark

Halt, adventurer, and read these words before you proceed!

You are about to embark on a journey. To where, only you could possibly say. It is not a journey like any you have been on before, where you start at page one and continue on a straight course until you reach the end. Instead, you will be presented with many choices along the way. Each time you are faced with one such choice, make your decision from the options given and then follow the directions to continue your adventure. Once your quest has come to an end, either favorably or, as I'm afraid in some instances it is foretold to, gruesomely, return to the beginning or the last choice and try again.

This is not a journey for those who prefer to sit back and let others make the tricky decisions. This is a journey for a leader, a true hero. One who is not afraid to converse with dragons, explore the Underdark, or face the dreaded two-headed Demogorgon. If this doesn't sound like you, turn back now and forget you ever came this way. But if this whiff of adventure has whet your appetite, then forward with you, my friend. And good luck!

CANDLEWICK
ENTERTAINMENT

DUNGEONS & DRAGONS®

ENDLESS QUEST®

ESCAPE THE UNDERDARK

MATT FORBECK

The last you remember, you were in a tavern, about to embark on your new career as an adventurer. A pale dwarf in a hooded cloak had sat you down to have a drink while he offered you a map to a dungeon he claimed was packed with treasure chests ripe for plundering.

But then the room got fuzzy and started to spin. You nodded off right there at the table, and the next you knew, you woke up here.

Only you're not exactly sure where *here* is.

It's cold, dark, and dank, and the floor is nothing but bare, roughhewn rock. So are three of the walls, but the fourth holds a heavy-looking door with a small barred window, just big enough to see out of.

You sit up, and the chains that connect the manacles on your wrists to the belt locked around your waist jangle. You swallow hard and realize that an iron collar is constricting your neck.

You groan, although you're not sure if it's from the pain in your head or the despair in your heart. As you do, a black-skinned male with long white hair and elven features—a drow, clearly, although you've never met one before—appears at the window in the door, a torch blazing in his hand.

"Finally awake, are you?" he says with a vicious grin that bares his sharp white teeth. "Welcome to Velkynvelve."

"Where?" A shiver runs down your spine as you realize just how much trouble you're in.

"The Underdark," a voice says behind you. You

spin around and see that you're not alone in your cage. In fact, there are several others trapped here with you: a deep gnome, an orc, a dwarf, and even a battered drow.

The dwarf was the one who spoke to you. The others don't even meet your gaze. "You're trapped in the Underdark," she says. "Enslaved by the drow."

"And there's no way out," the orc growls. "So don't bother trying to escape."

The guard laughs at the look of growing horror on your face and then walks away to let you stew in it. You scramble after him and grab the bars on the window of the

door. You try to rattle them, testing their strength, but they're as solid as the rock that surrounds you.

"Just like an orc to give up, Ront." The dwarf's voice drips with scorn.

The orc snorts at her. "Just like a dwarf to not know when she's beat, Eldeth."

"I'm not beat," you tell them all. "Not yet, at least. There has to be some way out of here."

The deep gnome laughs at you. "We're stuck in a giant spider-infested cavern a half-mile beneath the surface of Faerûn. None of us even know how we got here, and they work us so hard that the only thing we're good for afterward is sleeping it off."

"If you can find a way out, though, we'll follow," Eldeth says, her eyes brimming with her last bit of hope.

Bide your time. Turn to page 6 . . .
Fight! Turn to page 9 . . .
Escape. Turn to page 17 . . .

Rather than return you to your cell, Asha and Jorlan bring you to the door of Ilvara's office and remove the manacles from your wrists.

"Be quick about it," Asha says. "The faster, the better."

Jorlan hands you a knife, pats you on the back, and then pushes you toward the closed door.

"If you're caught, I'll tell Ilvara you stole that from me, so don't fail. If you do, she'll have me kill you for sure."

Grimacing at the unpleasant idea of your own death, you take your fate in your hands and slip into Ilvara's chamber. She ignores you, thinking that you're one of her subordinates, until your shadow falls across her. By the time she glances up it's too late. You plunge your knife into her chest and watch as she collapses over her desk, her mouth a small *o* of surprise.

A moment later, Asha bursts into the room to find you standing over Ilvara's corpse. She casts a spell that paralyzes you in your tracks. Suddenly, even breathing is incredibly difficult. You concentrate on keeping the rise and fall in your chest as you watch her move around the desk.

"Well done," she says as she inspects your handiwork, making sure that Ilvara is well and truly dead. "You saved me the trouble of having to move against her myself. Now the only question is what to do with you."

She stands before you with a worrying smirk on her face and gazes into your unblinking eyes. This is not how you saw this plan going.

"I might be able to convince my superiors that Ilvara was simply foolish enough to let you get close to her, but to let such an infraction by a slave go unpunished?" She shakes her head. "That would be too much for them to swallow."

You do everything you can to move even your eyelashes, but nothing works. The only thing you manage is to produce a bead of sweat that rolls down your cheek.

Asha reaches over and wipes it away. Then she steps back from you, well out of your reach, and begins to scream.

"Guards!" she yells. "Murder! Lolth's bloated thorax! Our leader has been murdered!"

As you hear the guards storm into the room, you know your days are over and there's not a single thing you can do about it.

THE END

You decide that the only way you're getting out of here is if you somehow pit your jailers against one another, and that sort of thing takes time. So you dedicate yourself to becoming a model prisoner, the kind that follows orders and causes no trouble. Every day you do whatever you're asked. When you return to your cell, you do so peaceably and without complaint.

You soon learn that your master is a female drow named Ilvara Mizzrym, a priestess of the spider goddess Lolth. Her top two lieutenants are a younger male named Shoor Vandree and a maimed older male named Jorlan Duskryn. They both vie for the favor of Ilvara and her assistant, Asha Vandree, although Shoor seems to have the advantage at the moment.

Shoor likes to beat the slaves and frequently promises to sell off those who fail to excel at whatever task he sets them. Jorlan seems not to care as much, but you suspect that's because he was once Ilvara's favorite. You learn that he lost that position to Shoor when an acidic ooze monster ambushed him in the darkness and ruined his handsome face, along with his right hand.

You manage to avoid angering either one of them, but you know that your time is running short. If you don't make your move soon, you'll be shipped off to Menzoberranzan, the great drow metropolis, and it might be impossible to escape from there.

"I wish all our prisoners were as easy as you," Jorlan says as he locks you back into your cell after a long day of dismantling and stacking rocks. "I'll miss you when they take you tomorrow. Most slaves are so hard to break in."

Ally with Shoor Vandree. Turn to page 12 . . .
Ally with Jorlan Duskryn. Turn to page 14 . . .

I refuse to live as a slave," you tell the others in your cell. "For me, it's freedom or death!"

"It's death for sure, then," the deep gnome says. "Might as well make it quick."

He sticks out his hand to you, and you shake it.

"Name's Jimjar," he says. "And I've got five gold pieces that say you can't break out of here today."

You squeeze his hand again, hard. "You're on."

Realizing that the more partners you have for your escape attempt the better, you turn to the dwarf. "You said you would help. Are you with us or would you prefer to rot here in this cell?"

"I'm with you," she says with a nod, though she seems less certain of her offer of help than she was before.

"Good. I need a distraction," you tell her. "Pretend I've gone mad and I'm trying to kill you."

She swallows hard and then lets out a tentative groan. "Ow! No! Stop!"

It's unlikely the guards have even heard her, much less that they will feel the need to investigate the disturbance. Ront leans over and smacks her across the cheek with an open hand. The slap echoes throughout the cell.

Eldeth screams in pain and clutches at the red handprint forming on her face.

"What are you doing?" the captive drow hisses accusingly at the orc, her eyes wide.

Ront shrugs. "Helping?"

You groan and wave Ront off while motioning for

Eldeth to keep screeching. As she complies with an ear-shattering howl, you position yourself to the side of the cell's door and wait for the sure arrival of your captors.

Soon enough, your drow jailer reappears and scowls at Eldeth through the barred window. "Keep it down in there!" he shouts, surveying the scene inside your cell.

"Help!" Eldeth cries as Ront advances on her again. "They're killing me!"

"None of that!" the guard says in a sharp voice. "You, orc! You keep your hands off our property!"

Ront slaps Eldeth again, cutting off her scream.

"Make me!" Ront taunts the guard, and you know that this is your moment.

The guard fumbles with his keys for a moment before unlocking the door. He charges in and points his sword at the orc.

"That's enough!" he demands, raising his eyebrows threateningly at Ront and adding a growl to his voice.

Wasting no time, you leap forward and level a haymaker at the guard from behind. As you swing your fist, though, your manacles haul you up short, blunting your blow.

You realize too late that you haven't thought this plan all the way through, and gulp in despair at what you now see is a failed escape attempt.

The guard spins around and slashes out blindly with his blade, forcing you back. Before you can press the attack, a host of other guards stream into the cell and begin beating you. They rain blow after blow down on you until you can't see, feel, think.

You awaken several days later with a splitting headache. It never goes away. You are able to follow orders from the guards, but that's as much as you can manage.

The guards set you to work tending the mushroom fields in a cave barely more than stumbling distance from your cell. You befriend a mushroom boy named Stool, whom you're not entirely sure isn't merely a product of your damaged brain. Despite that, his companionship makes you feel like it might just be okay that you never see the light of day again.

THE END

While you're working the next day, you manage to steal a moment alone with Shoor.

"Look," you say to the favored drow lieutenant, "I'm risking a lot by telling you this, but Jorlan came to me and asked me to kill you for him."

Shoor arches a white eyebrow at you. "Oh, did he?"

You're not sure that he's buying your story but it's too late to turn back now. What have you really got to lose in this godforsaken place anyway? Apart from your life, that is?

"He seems to think that you're the only thing standing between him and getting back into Ilvara's good graces."

"He's a fool," Shoor says, amused. "Even if he managed to get rid of me, Ilvara hates him. He'd be the next to go."

"Foolish? Or desperate?" you say. "You've backed him into a corner. What does he have left to lose?"

Shoor peers deep into your eyes. You will them not to give you away but apparently he doesn't like what he sees. Grabbing you by the collar, he hauls you over to have a little chat with Jorlan.

Turn to page 15 . . .

Jorlan hands you a knife and ushers you into Ilvara's office, closing the door behind you. Ilvara sits at her desk, writing a letter with a long white quill. When she looks up, she doesn't seem surprised to see you or the weapon glinting in your hand.

"Who sent you?" Her tone is both quiet and commanding at the same time.

"Asha. And Jorlan." You heft the knife in your hand.

"If you were going to kill me, you'd have already plunged that knife into my neck." She looks you over, sizing you up like you're a prize cow at market. "Your price for this job is your freedom? Do you really believe they will pay?"

"Will *you*?"

Ilvara shakes her head. "I let a slave go, and my people will think I've gone soft."

You step forward, and she rises to meet you. "I'll have Asha and Jorlan executed, of course," she says. "But you don't need to share their fate."

She reaches for the knife. "I'd rather you become my pet instead."

You hand her the knife and nod in agreement. You may remain a slave, but at least you'll be treated well for now.

THE END

T his doesn't have to be the end," you tell Jorlan.

He looks at you, suspicious. "How do you mean?"

"I notice the way Ilvara scorns you."

"There's nothing to be done about that."

"But what if she wasn't in charge?" You shrug in an offhand way. "What if someone else was boss around here?"

Jorlan dismisses your suggestion with a wave. "I know what you're thinking, but it won't work. In our society, the females are dominant. No one would follow me."

"Isn't there another female drow around here?" you say, knowing the answer. "Someone who might be better?"

Jorlan rubs his long chin for a moment, then unlocks your cell and beckons you to follow him. He takes you through a back passageway and introduces you to Ilvara's young female assistant, Asha.

Once he has relayed your message to her, she gives you a wicked smile. "I think you could be . . . useful."

Join Asha and Jorlan. Turn to page 4 . . .

Play along but betray them to Ilvara. Turn to page 13 . . .

S hoor hurls you at Jorlan's feet. "This slave claims you have a vendetta against me," he tells his rival.

Realizing that Shoor has betrayed you, you struggle to your feet and make a run for it. But you don't get ten feet before Jorlan knocks you down with a boot to your knee. He crouches on your back, grabs you by the hair, and sneers into your face.

"You think you're the first smooth-talking surface scum to try to set us against each other?" Jorlan spits at you. He smashes your face into the stone floor so many times, you find yourself hoping you'll pass out, which you soon do.

You wake up in Menzoberranzan, in the home of Ravel Xorlarrin, the wizard of House Xorlarrin.

"Excellent," Ravel says upon greeting you. "I hope you're healthier than the last few they sent me. The healthy ones tend to survive my experiments . . . for longer, anyway."

THE END

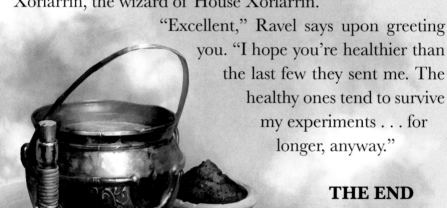

You decide to observe closely and seize the soonest chance to break out of your cage, but the next morning, Eldeth tells you that time is short.

"The guards say a merchant caravan is arriving from Menzoberranzan in a week or so. They'll take us all away!"

She hushes up when the guards come to escort you and the others off to your first day of work. They set you to breaking big rocks into smaller ones. When no one's looking, you grab a handful of gravel and stuff it into your pocket, a plan for escape starting to form in your mind.

Your arms are sore and your hands blistered when the guards haul you back to your cell. You stumble against the door as you enter and shove a chunk of gravel into the door's lock so it can't close properly. As the door clangs shut, you spin around and throw yourself against it to keep the guards from inspecting it.

The guards laugh as you reach for them through the barred window.

"A lot of spirit in that one," one of them says. "We'll have to beat it out of him."

You snarl at them, but they walk away laughing. Once they're out of sight and you can no longer hear their footsteps echoing around the passageways outside of your cell, you test the door and find that it swings free. The other prisoners gasp in amazement, but you silence them with a finger to your lips.

"Who's with me?" you ask.

"What about the guards?" Ront says.

"You'll never get past them," the battered drow prisoner, whom you've come to know is named Sarith, says with a chuckle. "Not without a distraction."

"Fortunately, there's one on the way," interjects the deep gnome, who's told you his name is Jimjar, as he steps forward, stroking his thin beard.

"What are you talking about?" Eldeth demands.

Jimjar shoots her a wary look. "I'm a scout."

"A spy, you mean," says Sarith.

Jimjar ignores him. "I was on my way back home to Blingdenstone when I was captured. The drow never would have caught me normally, but I was in a hurry to report in."

"Why?" You wonder what could scare Jimjar so much that he'd let himself stumble into a pack of drow slavers. "What news did you have?"

"Something is stirring deep in the Underdark," Jimjar says with a shiver. "Something evil."

"Heard rumors about that too," Ront says. "Some kind of demon war."

"What does that have to do with us?" you ask. You don't have long to make your way out of here, and you don't care to waste time on idle gossip.

"The war is boiling over," Jimjar says. "It's rising up through the Underdark."

"And you think it's going to reach here? Tonight?"

Jimjar shrugs. "Should have been here already. Might never come at all. Who's to know what's been planned in the deepest parts of the Underdark?"

"You're not much help."

"You're leaving either way, right?" Jimjar points at the door with his chin. "What's stopping you?"

You push on the door, and it swings open quietly on well-oiled hinges.

"Nothing," you say. "What's stopping the rest of you?"

The others stare at you and the open door for a long moment, then a horrible screech echoes in the distance.

Jimjar smiles and taps his ear. "Demons," he says. "Right on time."

"Now's our chance!" you tell the others. "Let's go!"

"We need to get rid of our shackles first," Jimjar says.

He pulls a lock pick from inside his cheek and sets to work. In a few moments, you're all free. Somewhere in the distance, drow soldiers shout, but the horrible screams only grow louder.

"We should go north!" Jimjar suggests as he bolts from the cell.

"To Menzoberranzan?" Ront says. "Forget it! South!"

"Toward Gracklstugh?" Eldeth shakes her head. "I'd rather take my chances with the drow than the duergar."

Jimjar chuckles at them. "Either way works for me, just as long as we get out of here." He looks to you to decide. "So, champ, which way is it?"

Head north, toward Menzoberranzan. Turn to page 26...

Head south, toward Gracklstugh. Turn to page 28...

Jimjar signals the guards, and the four of them surround you and usher you into the Darklake District of the city. They escort you to a gigantic cavern, which, unlike the rest of the Underdark, is well lit by scores of lamps and is as hot as an oven.

"This place is fueled by a red dragon," Jimjar whispers to you as the guards hand you off to another group of duergar.

They wear crimson priests' robes and regard you with a mixture of suspicion and hope. Their leader introduces himself as Gartokkar Xundorn and his group as the Keepers of the Flame, then explains that they have a problem.

Someone has stolen the egg of their dragon lord, Themberchaud. If you can recover it, they'll provide a guide to help you escape the Underdark.

From the next chamber comes a roar loud enough to shake the walls. "Enter, wayfarers!"

The four of you do so and come face to face with Themberchaud, red scaled and towering.

"Outsiders seem to be the only ones I can trust," he bellows. "You have been offered a deal, and I will have your answer now!"

Look for the thieves. Turn to page 31...
Refuse to help the dragon. Turn to page 33...
Play along for now. Turn to page 36...

You do your best to keep up with Jimjar, but he has too much of a head start on you. You lose the deep gnome in the darkness, and soon after that, you lose yourself as well.

You try to comfort yourself with the fact that you've escaped the drow, but the fact that you're alone and defenseless in the dark balances against that. As your eyes adjust, though, you realize that the Underdark isn't entirely dark. Bits of lichen on the walls give off a soft glow that's enough to walk by, if not run.

Still, that doesn't stop you from stumbling the moment the walls around you give way as the passage you're in opens wide into a gigantic cavern. You tumble off the edge of the cliff and shout in fear as you fall into the darkness.

You expect to fall to your death, but you instead find yourself caught in a massive spiderweb that stretches over the cavern's distant floor like a sticky net. You hope that whatever spun the web isn't near enough to have heard you and come looking to make you its prey.

Instead, a moment later, a pair of young goblins emerge from the darkness, sliding along the web on slippery feet faster than you could walk on it. They begin giggling at you. "You look lost," one of them says.

"Real lost," says the other. "Maybe we should let this poor human be, brother."

"No!" you say before they have a chance to leave. "You're right. I'm lost, and I need help finding my way out."

"What do you think, Yuk Yuk?" one of the goblins says to the other. "Sounds like it might not be boring, at least."

"Why not, Spiderbait?" the other one responds. "Unboring is good by me."

"All right," Spiderbait says with a grin. He points to the right. "That way's Menzoberranzan—which we won't have anything to do with. Those drow are too nasty!"

Yuk Yuk points to the left. "And that way's the Darklake. Which way is most unlost for you?"

Head toward Menzoberranzan. Turn to page 25 . . .
Head toward the Darklake. Turn to page 41 . . .

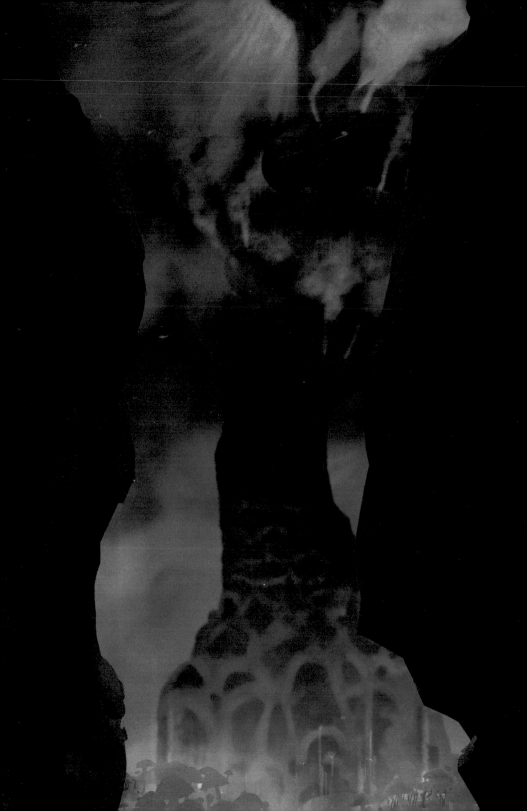

Everything I've heard about the Darklake is horrible," you tell the goblins. "I think I'll take my chances with Menzoberranzan."

"Then you're on your own," Spiderbait says, edging away from you.

"Good luck, human," Yuk Yuk says. "You're gonna need it."

With that, the pair disappear into the darkness. You struggle to your feet and get your balance on the web you're standing on, which is so thick it functions as a bridge across the chasm in which it hangs.

When you reach the other side, you walk in the direction of Menzoberranzan until you come upon a small garden of mushrooms. You lean over to inspect them, and one of them releases a puff of spores square into your face.

Soon after, the roof of the cavern above you opens, and you climb straight up to the surface. There you find your family waiting for you, and you're home safe and sound.

(You never realize you're actually hallucinating. Your mind may be free, but your body remains stuck in the Underdark until you happily waste away.)

THE END

N>orth it is!" you say as you emerge from the cell. "They'll never expect us to head toward Menzoberranzan."

" 'Cause it's a stupid idea," Ront says.

"I'm appalled to have to agree with an orc," Sarith says as he joins Ront in turning south.

"I thought for sure you'd join us," you tell the drow.

"There's nothing for me back home," he says with a bitter frown. "I was imprisoned here because I was accused of murder. The only thing waiting for me in Menzoberranzan is drow justice." He glances at Ront. "I'll take my chances in the wilds of the Underdark instead."

With that, he and Ront dash off in the other direction, leaving you with Eldeth and Jimjar. You gesture toward the deep gnome. "You're the scout here. Show us the way."

Jimjar sniffs the air and points to the east. "Brimstone. That means demons." Then he pads off to the north.

You follow close on his heels, and Eldeth trots after you. You hear the shouts and screeching fading in the distance as you move, and you begin to hope that there might be a chance for this day to end well for you after all.

Then an arrow lances out of the darkness and catches Eldeth in the chest. She screams in pain as she falls, and you spot a trio of well-armed drow guards charging your way.

Jimjar takes off at a sprint. You glance down at Eldeth, but she's already dead.

Another arrow spangs along the passageway, and you turn and chase after Jimjar as fast as you can.

Turn to page 22 . . .

S outh we go!" you say as you emerge from the cell. "I've had my fill of the drow. The farther away from Menzoberranzan, the better."

Eldeth shakes her head. "The duergar of Gracklstugh are no better. I wish you well, but I can't bring myself to go anywhere near there." With that, she turns and flees in the other direction.

You turn to Jimjar and give him a nod. "Lead on!"

The deep gnome flashes you a cocky smile and then heads off at a steady trot. You follow hot on his heels, and Ront and Sarith bring up the rear.

The sounds of battle grow more distant as you go, and you feel relieved that at least you didn't run square into whatever kind of fight is tearing apart Velkynvelve. Let them destroy one another while you find your way to freedom.

Jimjar leads you deeper into the Underdark. It takes days of travel to find the duergar city, and by the time you get there, you're thirsty and hungry and tired. But at least you're still free.

"Follow my lead," Jimjar says as you approach a checkpoint on the edge of the city. "The duergar are slavers too, but they're also pretty dumb."

"Wait," you say to the deep gnome. "What?"

But by then it's too late. The guards—gray-skinned dwarves, fully armed and armored—hail you and demand that you step forward. You exchange worried glances with Sarith and Ront, but, not seeing a better choice, the three of you follow Jimjar as he strolls toward the guards.

Turn to page 21 . . .

A t the end of the day, you and your three companions
bed down in a forest of glowing mushrooms that lights
up a large cavern, figuring you at least should have enough
to eat the next morning. Some of the mushrooms stand eight
feet tall, and as you're about to fall asleep, you realize that
the one right overhead is looking at you.

You shove yourself to your feet with a shout, and Ront,
Jimjar, and Sarith all leap up as well. Glancing around, you
see you're surrounded by giant mushroom creatures that are
all staring at you. Before you can run, several of them release
a puff of spores and you and the others set to coughing.

It's all right, a voice in your head says. *We mean no harm.*

"Neither do we!" you say. "We were just stopping to
rest for the night."

You're welcome to stay with us as long as you like, the voice
says. You're not sure if it comes from one of the mushroom
people—myconids, you remember they're called—or all of
them, but it's a generous invitation either way.

Stay awhile. Turn to page 50 . . .
Insist that they take you to the surface. Turn to page 54 . . .

You and your companions exchange "What choice do we have?" glances. "Of course we'll help," you pipe up.

Gartokkar Xundorn says he suspects that members of the local thieves' guild—the Gray Ghosts—either stole the egg or know who did.

"Then leave us to find them," you demand.

The priests allow you your freedom. They give you pins that mark you as protected by the dragon. "Just keep your eye out for anyone suspicious," they say.

The four of you set off. Most of the people in the city are duergar—gray dwarves—and they give you a wide berth, unaccustomed as they are to discourse with strangers. As you skulk about the place, doing your best to endure the excess heat from the fires Themberchaud provides to fuel Gracklstugh's legendary forges, you spy a derro. About the size of a duergar, he has bluish-white skin, and his eyes dance with madness.

Turn to page 34…

You try to back away from the dragon, but the heavy doors close behind you. You've never worked for a dragon before, but you've heard tales of those who have before—and they all seem to end with a fiery finish.

"I don't think we're well suited for this job," you try to tell Themberchaud.

"You don't refuse a dragon," Jimjar says with a hiss as the doors to the chamber slam shut behind you. "Ever."

Sarith tries to squirm his way behind you. "I have to agree with the human here, I think."

"I'm up for whatever doesn't get me eaten," Ront says, a note of rising panic in his voice.

"Fools!" the dragon roars. "I don't need your help. I don't need anybody! But nobody refuses me! Ever!"

You open your mouth to argue with the creature, to beg for mercy, to say anything to peacefully resolve the situation, but before you get three words from your mouth, the entire chamber fills with fire.

THE END

...s, you, Jimjar, Sarith, and Ront follow the derro ...at you suspect, by the abundance of faerzress, are ...stone Tunnels, listening as he argues with himself. The caverns are a series of dark, twisty tunnels that are easy to get lost in, but you do your best to follow quietly.

Eventually, you enter a brilliantly lit chamber with two low rocky shelves. On one stands a large black obelisk and on the other, a huge egg—the dragon's egg!

A humongous floating head with one big eye and four more on long eyestalks—a creature called a spectator—shrieks at you as you approach, and another derro tells you to stay where you are if you want to live.

"Look," you tell her, "we don't want any trouble. We don't even belong here."

She and the monster glare at you for a moment, and then she makes you an offer. She'll escort you to the surface—if you'll do her a favor.

Accept her offer. Turn to page 38...
Grab the dragon's egg instead. Turn to page 45...

You find a broken sword on the ground, snatch it up, and swing it at the translucent cube. The shattered edge slices through the thing's front side, and it lurches backward to avoid another strike.

Hey! the voice in your head shouts. *That hurt!*

"Come on, boys!" you say to the goblins. "Find us a way out of here while I hold this thing off!"

There really is no need to resort to violence, the voice says as the gelatinous cube edges away from you, leaving a trail of slime on the floor as it goes. *I am just trying to help!*

"This way!" Spiderbait says, waving at you from down a passage. With Yuk Yuk behind you, you back away warily, brandishing your broken weapon at the cube.

"We're clear," Yuk Yuk says. "Let's go!"

You spin on your heels and chase after the goblins. They're a lot faster than they look, even on their shorter legs, and you're all able to outdistance the cube in no time at all.

Careful out there! Glabbagool thinks after you. *It's dangerous for you fleshy types!*

Turn to page 55 . . .

You know better than to refuse a request from a fire-breathing mountain of scales. You also know better than to actually accept one. But that doesn't mean you shouldn't agree to work for him—and then run.

"We'd be honored to provide any assistance you might require," you say to Themberchaud.

"Of course you would." The dragon bares its teeth, each of which is as tall as you are. "My people will take you back to the city. However, once your task is complete, I require one additional thing from you."

"Anything you wish," Jimjar says. Ront and Sarith chime in to agree.

"You will report to me before you report to my underlings. No exceptions."

The dragon dismisses you then by closing his massive eyes. You hesitate for a moment, but when a gout of fire erupts from Themberchaud's nostrils, you take the hint and beat a trail toward the door.

"We'll get right on that," you tell the Keepers as you emerge from the dragon's personal chamber. "If you could just point us toward the closest way out of town . . ."

The priests take you to the nearest of the city's many gates. You head down the tunnel that leads beyond it, and once you're cleanly out of sight of Gracklstugh, you and your three companions sprint away.

If the Keepers or the dragon send someone after you, you never see them. You keep a good pace, though, still trying to find your way out of the Underdark.

Turn to page 30 . . .

There's a demonic cult that's taken up here in the Whorlstone Tunnels," the derro says. "Get rid of them, and I'll make sure you're taken care of."

You shrug at Jimjar, Sarith, and Ront. None of you really want to help out a dragon, and it seems as if this new task will be much less risky than chatting with Themberchaud again. You have the derro—who tells you her name is Pliinki—point you in the right direction, and you're off.

It doesn't take long for you to get lost in the caves again. When you stop and listen, you hear a group of people chanting. You can't make out everything they say, but the choruses of their chants all seem to center on the word "Demogorgon," which you recognize as the name of the prince of demons.

"Must be connected to the demons that attacked Velkynvelve," Jimjar says. "That's not good."

You and your companions creep closer, hoping to sneak up on the chanters. The passageway you're in widens out into a large chamber, and by the light of a campfire, you spot a natural platform at the far end of the room, on which stand a number of derro issuing the horrible chant.

Once you're all in the room, the derro turn toward you and screech something in a language you don't understand. The head priest points at something behind you, and you turn to discover a two-headed giant—an ettin—standing there, trapping you in the chamber with the cultists.

The ettin brandishes a gigantic spiked club at you, daring you to make a move. Ront takes it up on the challenge, and it smashes him into the rocks on which he stands. The rest of you put up your hands and surrender.

Turn to page 44 . . .

The two goblins run ahead of you, guiding you through the gigantic web-bridged chasm, which seems to go on for miles. There are moments when they disappear so thoroughly that you're sure they've abandoned you, but they always return a moment later, gliding in and out of the darkness to check and see if you're okay.

"Most people think the Silken Paths are crazy dangerous," Yuk Yuk says as he slides across the web on greased feet far faster than you can walk on it.

Spiderbait chuckles at that. "Sure, it's full of monsters, but what part of the Underdark isn't?"

"Just gotta know where to step!"

To their credit, the goblins do a great job of getting you safely across the chasm. Once you move back into the tunnels and caverns that make up most of the rest of the Underdark, though, it becomes clear that they're out of their depth. They stop and argue about which way to go several times, and in the end, they rely on your instincts to guide them. They're not the best navigators, but it's nice to have their company in this dark and scary place.

Soon enough, you find that the walls of the passageways through which you're creeping are damp. Some of them drip or even run with water. Hoping to stay dry, you try to not touch the walls as you go, but it is so tight in some places that you are soon soaked to the bone.

"Good sign," Yuk Yuk says. "We're getting closer to the Darklake!"

"Sure we're not under it?" Spiderbait asks. He's just

nervous enough to frighten you too, but you don't have much choice except to continue on.

Yuk Yuk giggles at your fear. "Don't worry about it," he says. "If the lake comes crashing down on us, we won't have any time to suffer!"

You repress the urge to snarl at the goblin and keep pressing on until the ceiling above you starts to creak. You stop in your tracks and raise your eyes to the ceiling. As you peer through the dim light, you can see a large crack already starting to form in the stones.

Spiderbait grabs you by the hand and hauls you along. "We gotta move," he says. "Fast!"

You nearly trip as he yanks you into motion but just manage to keep your footing. The creaking sound turns into a cracking noise and then a horrible rumbling you can feel all the way through your toes.

"Cave-in!" Yuk Yuk yells. "Run!"

You sweep both of the goblins up into your arms and charge forward as fast as you can. The ceiling begins to come down around you and for a moment you're sure this will be the end. Buried in the Underdark, no one will ever even hear of your daring escape from your captors.

You dash forward, dodging debris cascading from above. You come around a bend and see that the passageway you're in opens up into a small cavern.

"Move it!" Spiderbait shouts. "We can make it!"

You put one final surge of energy into your leaden legs and race forward. As you near the opening, the sound of the collapse becomes deafening. You dive toward the opening and sail through it just as the passageway behind you disappears in a cloud of rubble and dust.

As you and the goblins cough your lungs clear, you look up and spot a skeleton floating in the air before you, along with a sword and shield. They look like they should be falling to the floor along with the rubble that landed behind you, but they just hang there, suspended in . . . something. You start to back away, not too sure what this new horror is.

Then a voice sounds in your head—a voice that's not your own.

Greetings, it says. *I am Glabbagool.*

You realize then that the skeleton, sword, and shield are floating inside a transparent gelatinous cube!

Attack the cube! Turn to page 35 . . .
Make friends with Glabbagool. Turn to page 49 . . .

Pliinki appears, cackling in glee at how she betrayed you. She watches as the others tie you down in the center of the circle around which they were chanting. You struggle and protest, but it's no use. When Sarith starts shouting at them, promising them anything they want, the ettin shuts him up with a lethal blow from its club.

You and Jimjar gape at each other. "This is bad," he says. "Very, very bad. And not just for us."

"How could it get any worse?" you ask as the derro finish knotting you down and resume their chanting.

"They're about to sacrifice us to Demogorgon," Jimjar says. "And if that gets the demon prince's attention, he'll show up here and lay waste to all of Gracklstugh."

"You really think he's going to take on that dragon?"

Jimjar sighs. "I don't think we'll be around long enough to find out."

THE END

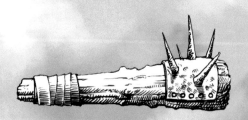

You knock over the derro guarding the dragon's egg and pick up the egg. You had no idea it would be so heavy!

A ray fires out of one of the spectator's eyestalks, and suddenly you can barely lift your arms, much less a massive egg. You drop it on the ground, breathing a sigh of relief when it doesn't crack.

Sarith picks up a rock and belts the spectator in its central eye. "That's how you deal with those!" he says.

The creature flies off, wailing in pain, and you feel the strength returning to your arms. With Ront's help, you pick up the egg again, and you all race out of the chamber.

As you go, the derro you knocked down stands up and starts shouting, "Gray Ghosts! Thieves have our treasure! Don't let them get away!"

You storm out of the Whorlstone Tunnels with what sounds like a small army of duergar and derro tramping after you. You glance back and see a dozen dirty thieves hot on your heels, each of them wielding a dagger they'd love to bury in your back. Wishing to do whatever you can to avoid that, you try to move quicker but the egg is heavy in your arms and you find it nearly impossible to pick up any sort of speed.

"We must hurry!" Jimjar says as he grabs the egg in the middle and tries to help move you along faster. "They're gaining on us!"

Sarith takes up a position on the side of the egg opposite Jimjar, and with the four of you working together, the egg doesn't seem so heavy.

You start to think you might be able to outdistance the Gray Ghosts after all. That's when the spectator comes flying over their heads, its main eye bloodshot and watery.

It fires off more rays from its eyestalks. One of them catches Ront square in the back, and you see the flesh on his

face erupt in blisters. The orc lets loose with a horrible howl of pain, but he keeps his hold on the dragon's egg and—just as important—keeps on running.

You race around a bend in the corridor, and you spot someone up ahead. A lot of someones.

At first you worry that they are a group of the city's guards who will attack because they're in too much of a hurry to see that you're wearing Themberchaud's pins. Then you realize that the people charging toward you are actually Keepers of the Flame!

"We're about to be in the middle of a big battle!" you shout to the others. "Which way should we go?"

"I say we give the egg to the Keepers!" Jimjar calls.

Sarith shakes his head. "Throw it back to the Ghosts!"

Ront laughs at them both. "Are you sure we can't just keep it for ourselves?"

Give the egg back to the Gray Ghosts. Turn to page 57 . . .
Keep the egg for yourselves. Turn to page 62 . . .
Give the egg to the Keepers of the Flame. Turn to page 65 . . .

You stand up and stare at the cube creature. In its depths, you spy a floating pair of eyes staring back at you.

"You can talk?" you say.

Telepathically, Glabbagool says.

"Can you hear it too?" you ask the goblins.

They nod wordlessly, gaping at the floating skeleton.

I mean you no harm, the gelatinous cube says.

"Tell that to whoever is floating inside you," says Yuk Yuk, disgust pulling at his lip.

Glabbagool quivers with regret. *He wouldn't stop attacking me. I had no choice.*

You clap the goblins on the shoulders and hold them steady in your grasp.

"Point us in the direction of the Darklake, and we'll be on our way," you tell Glabbagool.

Ooh, that's easy. Just follow me!

The creature moves slowly but surely through the passages, which are carved from the living rock, forming some kind of abandoned temple.

Turn to page 60 . . .

You, Jimjar, Ront, and Sarith settle down with the myconids, who treat you like royalty. They make sure you have plenty of fresh water to drink, and they bring you all you could ever want to eat—ensuring that you don't accidentally take a bite out of one of them.

Something about their means of communication—telepathy—makes you feel content. After spending a day with them, you wonder why you'd ever want to leave. The surface is hot and bright and dangerous, while here you're cool, safe, and have every need met. And it's so nice to have everyone around you know exactly what you mean without having to constantly explain yourself.

After the third day there, Ront tears himself away from the place, as does Sarith. You and Jimjar, though, decide to stay with the myconids and live in peace there for the rest of your lives.

THE END

You wind up shivering at the bottom of the chasm, suffering from a fever. The myconids gather around you, trying to offer what support they can.

You notice that they've done something to Ront. Soon after he died, they sprayed him with spores that have started to glow. A few of them have even formed little mushrooms on him like the kind you might see on the side of a tree.

As you watch, still shivering, Ront's body starts to twitch. A few minutes later, it manages to get up on its knees. It turns around and gazes at you with unblinking eyes as it pushes itself to its feet.

"What's happening?" you ask. "Is he . . . better?"

One of the myconids reaches out to wipe the sweat from your brow.

We have made him useful again. This is what we do to our kind. We bring them back into the cycle of life.

You're not sure whether you should be horrified or delighted. Either way you can't pass up an opportunity for escape so you ask, "Any chance he's useful enough to carry me out of this chasm?"

He is no stronger than he was before, and the walls of this chasm are very steep. He could climb out of here without you, but not with you.

Swallowing your disappointment and grimacing at the pain in your broken leg, you look up at the orc as he looms over you. "Ront?" you ask. "Can you hear me?"

The orc sways back and forth a bit. *Yes,* a new voice in your head says. Or so you think.

The idea that some bit of Ront continues on in this new, spore-powered form gives you hope. You might not ever make it out of the Underdark, but a new version of you might live on here. Possibly forever. Isn't eternal life something that most people only ever dream of?

"Is this how myconids are born?" you ask.

We are not born.

That sets you laughing, hard. Which sets you coughing harder. You can feel the end coming as you consider the company you have surrounded yourself with. All in all, there are definitely worse ways to go, you think, and soon you breathe your last breath.

Once you're gone, the myconids do the same thing to your body that they did to Ront's. They cover it with spores that quickly give your corpse a life of its own. Despite your broken leg, a few days later, your spore-powered form crawls out of the chasm and, with the help of Ront and the others, makes its way back to Neverlight Grove.

Jimjar and Sarith are happy to see you, even in your new state. They realize, though, that if they don't want to wind up like you, they'd better get moving soon. The next day, they depart from Neverlight Grove.

Jimjar comes back to check on you every now and then. He always leaves you with a wistful smile.

THE END

You like the myconids just fine, but you're wary of the spores they sprayed you with. Jimjar and Sarith decide to stay there in Neverlight Grove for a while, but the next morning, you and Ront insist that the myconids take you to the surface right away. Although they don't understand your decision—they love it here and never want to leave—they are only too happy to do their best to help.

A trio of myconids lead you out of Neverlight Grove, and you make good headway toward the surface. At one point, though, a rocky bridge you're standing on gives way, and you tumble into the darkness. The fall kills Ront instantly, and it leaves you at the bottom of a deep chasm with a broken leg.

The myconids manage to reach you, but they can't lift you out of the chasm. Your injury becomes infected, and you soon realize that you're not leaving the Underdark alive.

Turn to page 51...

You're looking back over your shoulder to see if Glabbagool is still following you, so you don't see Yuk Yuk and Spiderbait stop short when they spot something in front of them: a fountain filled with a gray substance that quivers in a way that an earthquake could never cause. You slam into them and knock all three of you over the lip of the fountain straight into the ooze.

Splashing up to the surface, you feel something slimy in your hand. You look down and see your broken sword dissolving into a bubbling liquid. Yuk Yuk opens his mouth to scream, and the ooze reaches up with a prehensile tendril and pulls the poor goblin under. Spiderbait never makes it back up.

You try to leap from the fountain, but more tendrils burst from the ooze and haul you down beneath its quaking, gray surface. Forever.

THE END

You skid to a halt and wait for the Gray Ghosts to catch up with you.

"Let's cut a deal!" you shout at them as they get closer. "You can have the egg back, and we'll just step aside and let you deal with the Keepers!"

The Gray Ghosts answer only with their blades. They leap at you, snarling and howling for blood.

A slash from one knife hamstrings Ront, and he falls to the ground. There are now only three of you holding the egg, which seems solid enough to maybe crack the floor rather than the other way around. You lose your grip on it too, and it rolls a few feet away before coming to a rest between you and the oncoming crowd.

You realize you've made a terrible mistake, but it's too late to do anything about it. You're certainly not going to risk your life retrieving it now. The best you can hope for is to hold on long enough for the Keepers of the Flame to reach you before the Gray Ghosts kill you all.

A vicious pair of derro come after Sarith. One of them slashes at his knee, and while Sarith is dancing away from the blow, the other derro thrusts a knife into his belly. He falls, clutching his wound.

A trio of Gray Ghosts storm Jimjar. They knock him over, and he tumbles beneath them in tangle of limbs and steel. You hear him shout some kind of warning—or perhaps he's trying to make one last deal—but he's cut off by a horrible gurgling sound.

With all of your companions down, you stand alone

against the spectator, which flies straight over the fallen egg and zaps you with a ray from one of its eyestalks. It catches you in the chest, and you feel a strange paralysis spread across your entire body in an instant. You struggle to move, but no part of you is able to. Even breathing is difficult,

and blinking is completely out of the question. You wonder whether things could get much worse when the spectator zips straight down in front of you and waves the Gray Ghosts off with its eyestalks. "This one," it says in a gravelly voice, "is all mine!"

The Gray Ghosts keep their distance from the spectator, but the Keepers of the Flame charge straight at it. One of them lets loose with a spectral hammer that comes sailing straight at the spectator's central eye. When the spectator stares at it, though, the hammer turns around and attacks the Keepers instead. Doomed seems to be an understatement as Keeper after Keeper falls under the spectator's attack.

"I'll hold them off!" the spectator says to the Gray Ghosts. "Get the egg!"

You can't even turn your head to see the Ghosts, but you can hear the egg rolling across the rocks as they move it away. You wonder if you'll make the same sound when you're rolling in your grave.

THE END

Eventually, you and the two goblins, led by the cube creature Glabbagool, reach a larger chamber with a hole in the ceiling, through which water is pouring.

Once the chamber floods, Glabbagool explains, *you should be able to swim out of here!*

It seems to take forever but you wait until the chamber fills with water, and then swim to the hole in the top. You can reach the ceiling just fine, but you have to boost the goblins up. Once they're safe, you climb out after them.

The Darklake should be close, Glabbagool thinks at you. *Just follow the water!*

"Thanks for your help," you say to the gelatinous cube. "I'll never forget you!"

Nor I you! After all, you're the only person I've ever met who hasn't tried to kill me!

You try not to think too much about that as you follow the goblins, who have already scampered into the darkness. You find them sitting on the shore of a vast underground lake that seems to stretch forever. It could almost be pretty if you weren't so desperate to get out of this place.

"We're stuck," Yuk Yuk says.

"Nothing but water behind us, and nothing but water ahead," says Spiderbait.

Realizing that the goblin brothers are right, you sit down next to the goblins and stare out at the water, waiting for your eyes to adjust to the darkness and considering your options. There are things in the water that glow softly and move with a slow and sinuous grace. Beautiful as they are, you can't help but wonder if they might eat you if you try to swim for it.

The goblins tense and dig their fingers into your arms.

"Ow! Stop it!" you cry.

"Look," Spiderbait whispers. "It's right there!"

You squint into the darkness and see a silhouette outlined against the glowing things in the water. It's vaguely human shaped but with the head of a gigantic fish. It rises out of the Darklake and approaches you slowly.

"Greetings, air-breathers," it says in a burbling voice. "I am Plooploopeen of the kuo-toa who call the Darklake home. You seem lost."

You don't see any reason to lie about that. "Can you help us?" you ask.

"Of course," Plooploopeen says. "But only if you'll help me take over my hometown."

Of course, do anything! Turn to page 69 . . .
Don't trust the creature. Turn to page 71 . . .

You spy a passageway off to your left and dart into it, leading the others.

"What in the name of all the forgotten gods are you doing?" Sarith shouts at you.

"Getting away from being stuck in the middle of a battle!" you shout back.

"But where are we going?" asks Ront.

"Anywhere but there!"

"I've got ten gold pieces that say we don't make it out of this alive," says Jimjar.

"And if you win, how are you going to collect on that?" Sarith says with a sneer.

"Right . . ." Jimjar says. "Better make it twenty."

You ignore Jimjar and keep charging ahead through the tunnels, turning this way and that in an effort to throw off your pursuers. A huge roar resounds behind you as the Keepers of the Flame clash with the Gray Ghosts. You can hear some of the combatants peel off and come after you, ignoring the larger fight. You need to get out of here, and quickly, otherwise Jimjar really may be collecting on his twenty gold in the next life.

"Keep running!" you call to the others.

Ront refuses. He drops his side of the egg, and the rest of you readjust to compensate and keep it from rolling out of your hands. You open your mouth to shout at him, not understanding why he would choose to opt out of the heavy lifting, now of all times.

"Go!" he shouts at you. "I'll take care of them!"

You would love to protest Ront's bravery, but you don't have time. Instead you set your lips into a grim smile and give him a nod of thanks before you set off again. The journey is more challenging with one fewer person to share in the burden of the egg. At least there's more time to find your way through these passages, though the cost is too high for your liking.

"He's been spoiling for a fight ever since we escaped our cell," Sarith says, as though that makes it okay that you have left a man — or orc in this case — behind.

"Looks like he got one!" says Jimjar.

You hear the orc growl like a hungry bear, and somewhere behind you, a pack of duergar let loose with horrified screams. You're grateful to Ront for helping you lose your pursuers, but you wonder how he'll ever manage to find you again. You just can't worry about that detail right now. All you can concentrate on is putting one foot in front of the other and finding a way out of here.

Turn to page 68 . . .

The four of you—you, Jimjar, Sarith, and Ront—put on a burst of speed and find yourselves in the midst of the Keepers of the Flame.

"We have the egg!" you shout at them.

"We can see that!" their leader says. "Keep it safe!"

At his command, the other Keepers fan out and get ready to face the Gray Ghosts while you find yourself surrounded by three of the Keepers who escort you to safety. The battle breaks out behind you as you make a speedy exit.

"Even if the thieves carry the day, we're not going to let them take the egg again!" the leader shouts after you as you plunge deeper into Gracklstugh.

Your escorts bring you to the nearest gate and call on the guards there to give them a hand. If you had any thoughts of trying to run off with the egg, they disappear. Instead, you let the guards bring you a cart, into which you set the egg.

The Keepers offer to push the cart from there, but Jimjar's not about to let them.

"They just want to take all the credit when we get back to the dragon," he explains. "We didn't risk our lives for that to happen."

When you get to the Keepers' headquarters, though, your escorts won't let you go in to see the dragon alone.

"It's simply too dangerous," they explain. "He ate the last person who dared enter his chamber without our leader, Gartokkar Xundorn, giving his blessing beforehand."

"Where is Gartokkar now?" Sarith asks.

"The last I saw of him, he was attacking that spectator who was with the Gray Ghosts," the Keeper says.

You cool your heels outside Themberchaud's chamber for what seems like an hour, becoming increasingly impatient at the delay in putting an end to all of this. Eventually, Gartokkar arrives. His uniform is slashed and bloodied in several places, but he appears to be unharmed.

"The Gray Ghosts nearly killed us all," he reports with a grim smile. "But we drove them off in the end. And here's one of the benefits of knowing healing magic." He taps at a fresh scar on his face. "It doesn't hurt for very long, at least."

He regards the egg in the cart and the door to the dragon's chamber.

"He hasn't demanded you go in to see him yet?"

You shake your head.

"Excellent. Better, I think, if he never realizes you were involved in this. He has a tendency to become angry with anyone who handles one of his eggs without first undergoing the proper rituals. That said, we're extremely grateful to you for the return of the egg, and we will be happy to make good on our promise."

He glances at each of you in turn, and you immediately realize that he's lying about the dragon. You're not sure you should care.

Gartokkar continues. "I believe that involved an escort from here to a safe location on the surface. We are also willing to provide a suitable reward and whatever armor and weapons you might need in order to guard it."

Accept the Keepers' offer. Turn to page 75 . . .
Insist on an audience with the dragon. Turn to page 77 . . .

You, Sarith, and Jimjar round one last bend and emerge into a blazing-hot cavern. At the far end glows the fires of one of Gracklstugh's massive forges, and duergar work over a pool of molten metal. Startled by your entrance, they take one look at you and scatter. You let them weave their way around you. Unlike Ront, you're not looking for a fight.

You hear shouts echoing back the way you came. "I think they're still after us," you tell the others.

"There's no other way out of here," says Sarith. "We're trapped."

"We still have the egg," says Jimjar. "That has to be worth something. We can use it as a bargaining chip, right?"

Sarith scowls at him. "Or we can threaten to toss it in the fire if they don't let us go."

You feel the weight of the egg in your hands. You don't have long to make up your mind.

Threaten to throw the egg into the forge. Turn to page 78...
See if you can cut a deal. Turn to page 84...

You don't want to get involved in kuo-toan politics, you don't see how you have much of a choice. You no___ your agreement, and Ploopploopeen shows you a wide-mouthed grin that displays rows of small sharp teeth.

"Excellent," the fish man says. "Then, as part of a grand ruse, I will bring you into our city, Sloobludop, as my prisoners, and I will allow you to be sacrificed on the Altar of the Deep Father."

"I don't like this plan," Yuk Yuk says, and you don't blame him.

Ploopploopeen dismisses the goblin's protest with a wave of a finny hand. "There's no need for concern. You will not be harmed. Once you are in place, you simply need to fight back against the guards there. I will take advantage of that distraction to launch a coup against our leaders and my daughter."

"Sounds dangerous," Spiderbait says. "And tricky."

"Far less dangerous than sitting out here on the edge of the Darklake," Ploopploopeen says. "Or trying to cross the waters on your own." He puts his slimy hands on his hips. "If I wished to harm you, I could easily just kill you here and now. Or I could wait for you to die on your own."

Ploopploopeen gazes into your eyes with his wide, black orbs. "You help me out now, and I'll help you later. You have my word."

"All right," you say. The goblins both object, but you shush them fast. "We don't have much of a choice."

"Wise decision," Ploopploopeen says, flashing his

again. "I'll be right back with a boat for you, and
immediately."

the kuo-toan is gone, you reassure the goblins
ot blindly trusting him. "Just be ready to follow
my lead," you tell them.

Soon after, you find yourself slipping into the town
of Sloobludop on little more than a wooden raft towed by
Plooploopeen. "Ahoy, the town!" he shouts as the raft brings
you in. "I have captives!"

A group of warriors line the dock and eye you warily
as they greet their leader.

Go along with the plan. Turn to page 82...
Betray Plooploopeen. Turn to page 86...

Go along with the plan. Turn to page 82...
Betray Plooploopeen. Turn to page 86...

but

You look Ploopploopeen up and down and decide you can't trust a strange fish person who emerges from an underground lake to cut you a deal.

"I think we'll do just fine on our own," you tell him.

He shrugs. "Suit yourself. I'll come back to ask again. If you're still here, you might be . . . hungrier for a bargain. Although the terms might not be as good."

Spiderbait chucks a rock at the kuo-toan, and it bounces off his scaly skin. He takes the hint and slips beneath the lake's surface, which soon is so smooth again that you would think no one had been there at all.

"And now we're stuck," Yuk Yuk says. "Nice work."

"There has to be another way out of here," you tell the goblins. "We could swim."

"You see those glowing things in the depths?" Yuk Yuk says. "They look hungry to me."

"Maybe we could build a raft," Spiderbait says.

"Out of what?" Yuk Yuk shakes his head at how dense his brother is. It seems as though he would rather sulk on the banks of this lake forever than offer any solutions to your predicament himself.

"Didn't we pass a grove of massive mushrooms a little way back?" you say. "Maybe we could find something there."

Intent on investigating the options, you start off back in the direction you came from. Spiderbait follows right behind and Yuk Yuk reluctantly brings up the rear. The passage opens onto a cave filled with mushrooms of all shapes and sizes. One in particular has a cap that's as large as a bed.

"We could use that as a raft!" Spiderbait points it out to you in excitement.

"As long as it doesn't tip over in the middle of the lake," Yuk Yuk says.

"I don't see anything that'll work better," you say. "Come on, it's worth a try at this point. What other option do we have?"

With a little difficulty, you and the goblins snap the top of the mushroom off and roll it back through the passage until you reach the lake.

You slip the giant mushroom cap into the lake's chilly waters, and to your great delight and astonishment, it floats! The goblins give out a cheer, and you join them, clapping them on their backs in celebration.

You hold the cap steady as Spiderbait and Yuk Yuk climb aboard, and then you shove it away from the shore and slip onto it yourself. Then you and the goblins dip your hands into the

water and start paddling. It's clumsy and slow, but it works.

"Where are we going?" you ask the two goblins, hoping they have some ideas.

"We could follow that kuo-toan," Yuk Yuk says. "I saw him swimming along the shore—although that might lead us into trouble with his gang."

"Or we could steer clear of all that and go straight across the Darklake," says Spiderbait.

Yuk Yuk groans. "Where we might tip over and drown in the deepest part."

They both look to you for guidance. You rub your chin and consider the options.

Head across the Darklake. Turn to page 90 . . .
Follow the shore. Turn to page 92 . . .

True to his word, Gartokkar has the Keepers outfit you and each of your compatriots with a brand-new set of armor, a razor-sharp sword, and plenty of food and drink for your trip, as well as a small sack filled with gold and jewels. They also use their magic to ensure that you and the others are as healthy as can be.

"We are forever indebted to you," the high priest of the Keepers of the Flame says. "By the same token, I hope—for your sakes—that we never see you again."

You, Sarith, Ront, and Jimjar can only laugh and agree with that sentiment. After a good night's rest, you set off for the surface with a trio of Keepers as your guides.

As you get closer to the surface, though, your companions begin to get nervous.

"I've got no one to go back to," says Ront. "I got lost in the Underdark after the rest of my war band got slaughtered by dwarves we'd been attacking."

"I can't go back to Menzoberranzan either," says Sarith. "I'm accused of murder there."

"One you didn't commit?" you ask.

"I never said that."

You turn toward Jimjar. "What about you?"

He chuckles. "I'm always welcome back home in Blingdenstone." He hefts his treasure sack. "At least I will be if I return with enough of this to pay my debts." He glances at the others. "But where would be the fun in that?"

Once the Keepers leave you on the surface, you spend a few days with the others recovering and enjoying the sun.

"You know," says Jimjar, "I have a map to a dungeon that needs exploring. I think it's not too far from here."

"And we have all this equipment now," says Sarith.

"Seems a shame to let it go to waste," says Ront.

They turn to you, and you give them a big smile.

THE END

W e're not going anywhere without seeing Themberchaud," you inform the Keepers. They try to keep you from entering the great beast's chamber, but, at the sound of you scuffling with them outside his door, he lets loose a mighty roar.

"Have my emissaries finally returned?" he shouts through the door. "See them in now! And bring my egg!"

Shaken by their master's wrath, the Keepers fling open the door and escort the four of you into the dragon's overheated chamber. They push the cart carrying the dragon's egg in behind you, then close the heavy door.

"How did you know we had your egg?" Ront asks.

"Only suicidal fools would have returned without it," the dragon says, baring all of his vicious teeth. "For that you have my gratitude. And especially for not letting my underlings keep it from me. They think I don't know, but they plan to use that egg of mine to replace me once I become too unbearable for them to deal with."

Turn to page 81 . . .

On the count of three, you, Sarith, and Jimjar position the egg over the molten metal pooled in a stone basin at the edge of the forge. But as you wait for your pursuers to catch up, the egg stirs in your hands. In alarm, all three of you let go, and it splashes into the glowing-hot pool. You barely manage to dodge out of the way of the liquefied steel.

Horrified, you stare at the egg, wondering just how long it will take for it to burn, but it doesn't seem to be catching fire. In fact, it's starting to glow.

A moment later, the egg bursts open, sending scorching-hot shards of shell everywhere. You duck away from the shrapnel, then immediately pop up again to see what happened to the egg.

A baby dragon sits among the remnants of the exploded egg, and it stares up at you with wide, questioning eyes that lock on yours. Its lips curl up in what you can only believe is a smile, and it lets out a cry that sounds something like joy.

The dragon leaps from the forge and lands in your arms. It's so hot that it almost burns you, but the creature's skin quickly cools as it begins to lick your face.

A team of Gray Ghosts, cut and bloodied, burst into the chamber and gasp at you in horror.

You turn toward them, holding the wriggling dragon out before you.

"This isn't what it seems."

"You hatched the dragon?" one of the Ghosts says.

"Okay," says Sarith. "It's *exactly* what it seems."

The Gray Ghosts storm toward you, and the dragon lets out a gout of fire that burns them all in their tracks. Those that don't fall down screaming turn tail and flee. As you move toward the exit, the dragon lets loose with its fiery breath again, and soon the chamber is empty of enemies.

"I think we just found our ticket out of here," Jimjar says. He reaches out to pet the dragon but leaps back when the creature nips at his fingers.

You proceed out of the chamber and head straight into the Underdark, carrying the heavy little dragon in your arms. With the dragon's help, nothing can stand in your way. You commandeer a wheelbarrow to cart the dragon around in and resume your trip upward. Within a few days, you finally make it to the surface. Once you're out in the open air, the dragon takes off into the sky to stretch its wings.

"Think it's ever coming back?" you ask the others.

Nobody answers. It doesn't matter. You're all free now.

THE END

Why do you think the duergar keep me here?" Themberchaud says. "I was born in this chamber. I grew up here, stoking the flames of their forges since I was little more than a hatchling, the same as my forebears. And now I am far too large to ever leave. Even if I tore the entire place down around me, I could not claw my way to the surface from here. Instead, I remain buried in a prison of my parents' making, far beneath a sky I've never seen."

"We've all been prisoners," you say, suddenly sympathetic to the massive beast.

"But now, for the first time in my life, I have the upper claw," the dragon says as he reaches out and strokes his egg with a yard-long talon. "They can't get rid of me without a replacement. They cannot risk the fires of their forges going out. But if I have the egg when it hatches, the dragon inside will be loyal to me, and they will not be able to convince it to take part in my undoing. For returning my insurance of safety to me, you have my undying thanks."

He stares at you with a gigantic eye. "I've instructed Gartokkar to reward you well in addition to escorting you to the surface. We shall not meet again." And with that, he turns his back to you in dismissal.

Gartokkar keeps the dragon's word, equipping you, Jimjar, Ront, and Sarith with the finest armor and weaponry and escorting you out of the Underdark. You can hardly believe it, but at long last you are free.

THE END

Ploopploopeen brings you and the two goblins to the Shrine of the Sea Mother, which looks like someone took apart a giant crayfish and used it to decorate a nine-foot-tall statue. "Gaze at her beauty," he says. "She shall save us all."

"Sacrilege!" cries another kuo-toan, arriving with a large force of warriors. "Such outsiders belong not to the Sea Mother but the Deep Father!"

"You dare too much, daughter!" Ploopploopeen says. "You cannot have these warm-bloods for your evil sacrifices!"

"And you cannot stop progress!"

Ploopploopeen sticks out his lower lip as if he is considering the situation. "Fine, Bloppblippodd," he says to his daughter. "Take them, and may your Deep Father choke on them."

Bloppblippodd and her warriors escort you and the goblins to a shrine made of a pair of dead octopuses tied together atop a dead manta ray that's stretched over a hide covering a low altar.

"Ewww," Spiderbait says with a shudder. His brother shushes him, but you can see that Yuk Yuk is shivering too.

As Bloppblippodd is bringing you

up to the stinking altar, Ploopploopeen steps forward and clobbers her over the head. The warriors on his side level their spears at her supporters and attack!

You kick one kuo-toan over, snatch away its spear, and then enter the fight yourself. An enemy warrior charges at you, but you tackle him onto the altar and pin him there with the spear. For a moment he looks at you in horror, but as his blood starts to spill onto the altar, a smile plays on his lips, sending a shiver down your spine. You turn from him to find a full-on battle raging around you, pitting kuo-toa against one another.

Yuk Yuk and Spiderbait are hiding behind the altar, and you stand guard over them, keeping them safe from the brawl. The warriors are all too busy with one another to pay any attention to you.

Just as Bloppblippodd comes to, rises on wobbly legs, and turns toward you, a horrifying rumbling comes from the direction of the Darklake.

Turn to page 89 . . .

The three of you put the egg down, sit on top of it, and wait. You're all too tired to run any longer. There's nothing to do now but await your fate.

A group of Gray Ghosts storm into the room and accost you. "Give us the egg!" they demand.

"You're welcome to it," you say as you and your companions slide off it. "If you can keep it."

You, Sarith, and Jimjar back off to the farthest corners of the cavern as the Gray Ghosts pick up the egg. As they hoist it onto their shoulders, a platoon of Gracklstugh's guards appears in the doorway.

"Hold it right there!" their leader barks.

The guards stream into the room and arrest all three of you. You try to tell them that you're working with the Keepers of the Flame, but they don't believe you until they see Themberchaud's pin still stuck to the front of your shirt.

"Get them to the king," the leader says.

The next thing you know, you, Sarith, Jimjar, and the egg are lifted by dozens of unseen hands. These invisible people carry you from the forge and through the winding ways of Gracklstugh until you reach the Hold of the Deepking. Before you rises a dark stone structure stuck between two massive natural stone columns, stabbing upward toward the ceiling above, which is masked by thick clouds of smoke. It is all underlit by a hellish glow from the forges that surround the tower.

The invisible guards haul you through the front gates and into the central hall, which is lined by cataracts of lava tumbling between black columns of basalt. The invisible guards set you down before the iron throne at the far end of the hall, upon which sits a gray-skinned duergar dressed in thick robes and an ornate iron crown.

Turn to page 93...

A force of kuo-toan warriors escorts you and the goblins from the shores of Darklake into Sloobludop proper. Ploopploopeen takes you to the Shrine of the Sea Mother, where he promptly vomits the contents of his stomach onto the feet of a nine-foot-tall wooden statue of a woman with the head and forearms of an actual giant crayfish strapped into place upon it.

"The sea goddess Blibdoolpoolp is a scavenger, so she appreciates best the things we leave behind for her. Do you wish to make an offering yourself?"

"I thought we *were* the offering," Spiderbait says softly.

Ploopploopeen smiles. "To another god—a false one—shortly. Wait for it."

Another kuo-toan arrives then, with an even larger force of warriors at her side. "Father! You dare offer these people up to the Sea Mother?" she says to Ploopploopeen.

"I claim them for the Deep Father instead! Guards, take these sacrifices."

"I forbid it, Bloppblippodd," Ploopploopeen says.

Unnerved by the vomiting, you turn and point at Ploopploopeen. "This one is trying to trick you! We're supposed to help attack you!"

"Traitor!" Ploopploopeen shouts as he throws himself at you. The guards with Bloppblippodd step between you and him, keeping you safe. While holding Ploopploopeen at spear-point, they grab you and the goblins to haul you away.

"Wait!" you plead. "I just saved you from treachery. All we want is our freedom! Is that so much to ask?"

"Not at all," Bloppblippodd says. "And you shall have it immediately. To be free from the absolute madness of life. Isn't that what we all deserve?"

"But we helped you!" Yuk Yuk says.

"And for that, I shall give you the best gift of all, warm-blooded ones," Bloppblippodd says. "A quick death."

THE END

He is risen!" Bloppblippodd shouts as she stabs a long slimy finger toward the most distant parts of the Darklake. "Leemooggoogoon has come!"

"What's a Leemooggoogoon?" Spiderbait asks as he and Yuk Yuk cling to your legs.

You peer into the darkness, and somewhere out there, you see a hellish light erupt from the water. Another one follows it soon after, and the two lights move in sync with each other, like two glowing eyes floating in a gigantic skull.

As the humongous beast grows closer, it slaps at the water with two tremendous tentacles, each split about halfway down. Soon you can see that the two lights are actually mouths set in twinned heads, each glowing from the fires burning within the belly of the shared torso.

"Demogorgon," you say. "They mean Demogorgon. According to my sources back home, he's a demon prince from the Abyss. And the kuo-toa have just summoned him."

This must be what brought the demons to Velkynvelve, you realize. Demogorgon has been preparing to attack the Underdark for a while. And now you're right in his path.

Fight! Turn to page 94 . . .
Flee! Turn to page 98 . . .
Trick him! Turn to page 108 . . .

You paddle the mushroom cap farther and farther across the Darklake, leaving the shore in the darkness behind you. After a while, you realize that you couldn't make your way back to shore even with a knife at your throat.

You've been at it for at least an hour when you feel something bump up against the bottom of the mushroom cap hard enough to make the entire thing shudder. Spiderbait nearly tumbles into the water, but you grab him by the arm to steady him before he falls.

"What was that?" Yuk Yuk asks, the pitch of his voice climbing in terror.

You look around in panic and spot the tip of a softly glowing barbed spear sticking up through the mushroom cap. Another foot over, and it would have stabbed you in the belly.

"Paddle, boys!" you tell the goblins. "Paddle hard!"

The three of you lean into it, splashing and hauling your way through the water with as much strength as you can muster.

"Are we going anywhere?" Spiderbait asks.

"We're being pulled under!" Yuk Yuk shouts.

You realize the goblin is right. Your makeshift raft has been swamped, and you're sinking fast.

The goblins dive into the Darklake and start swimming. You curse their impulsiveness. Where there's one harpoon thrown at you, there are sure to be others, and once you go into the water, it's doubtful that you'll ever come out.

Still, you don't have any choice. You dive into the

water, which closes above you, and swim hard toward Yuk Yuk and Spiderbait.

You only make it a few strokes before a harpoon pierces your chest and starts to haul you under too. You fight until the blackness takes you, hoping at least the goblins might manage to get away. . . .

THE END

You paddle along the shoreline, keeping to the shadows, and soon you come upon a half-submerged city festooned with glowing towers stabbing from the shallows. You hope you might be able to find someone there to help you, and your heart rises when a kuo-toan emerges from the waters nearby.

Your heart drops again when you see there's not just one kuo-toan but a full dozen of them.

"It's Plooploopeen!" Yuk Yuk shouts.

You stand and wave at Plooploopeen. "I'm afraid we got off on the wrong foot," you tell him.

Spiderbait taps you nervously on the leg. "I think you mean 'fin,' right?"

Plooploopeen shouts something in a fishy language you don't understand, and the kuo-toan warriors rush forward to attack, tridents in hand. You try to explain that it's all just a big mistake, but it's too late!

THE END

K neel before King Horgar Steelshadow the Fifth!" an unseen crier shouts. You, Sarith, and Jimjar do as you're ordered. Although he's far shorter than you, the king towers over you from the dais on which his throne sits.

"You outsiders who dare defile my halls!" he says.

You start to protest, but an invisible hand slaps your face and another clamps over your mouth to keep you silent.

"I thank you for your service and your sacrifice. With Themberchaud's egg returned to us, the future of our forges is secure!"

A roar of approval goes up from the invisible guards.

"In gratitude for your accomplishment, I will not execute you on the spot. I welcome you into my kingdom as ambassadors from the surface world—permanently."

"We accept your kind offer," you tell the king.

"How cute!" he says with a sinister laugh. "You thought that was an offer. . . ."

THE END

Y ou're tired of running in the dark even in the face of such horror. If Demogorgon wants a fight, he's going to get one!

The bulk of the kuo-toa panic. Those following Bloppblippodd, however, raise their arms to the sky in a gesture of triumph.

"Leemooggoogoon has come to conquer the world!" she cries. "As his chosen people, we will bask in the glory of his madness!"

As far as you can tell, the madness has already infected Bloppblippodd and her cult of followers. Only insane people would summon the prince of demons to their home.

Plooploopeen isn't doing much better, though. He's fallen to his knees and is gibbering in fear, along with most of his followers. You can hardly blame him, but that's not going to get any of you out of this situation alive.

You stride over and smack Plooploopeen across his gills. The blow seems to bring the kuo-toan to his senses, and he stares up at you with wide, unblinking eyes.

"Get it together!" you say to him. "I can't fight this monster alone!"

"Right!" Plooploopeen says. "My kuo-toa! Devotees of the Sea Mother! This is our moment! We must unite against the great evil that storms our home! We must fight!"

You snatch up a discarded spear and hurl it at Demogorgon. To your great astonishment—and slight horror—the shaft arcs out over the waters of the Darklake and finds its mark! It buries itself in Demogorgon's shoulder, and the demon prince hauls back both of his baboon-like heads and howls in pain.

The roar is enough to shake the entire cavern. Stalactites rain down from the unseen roof like stone missiles, and the two goblins take refuge underneath the shrine's horrifying altar.

Heartened by your success, Plooploopeen's warriors begin to hurl spears at Demogorgon as well. A dozen shafts arc through the sky and strike true.

The demon prince, however, plucks several of the spears from his hide and brushes off the rest. They've done little more than irritate him.

You wonder what chance you can possibly have against such a foe as this and consider running. Your doubts at success only increase when Bloppblippodd sends her

warriors to attack those of her father. They charge forth and meet Ploopploopeen's army with an almighty crash.

"Stop them!" she cries. "Show our Deep Father how he can count on us to protect him from these heretics!"

Demogorgon rushes up out of the waters of the Darklake, and you're sure he doesn't need any help at all. He stands at least three times as tall as you, and as he lays about with his tentacles and his gigantic forked tail, nothing manages to stand before him. Homes fall, towers crash, people scream.

As the kuo-toa fall into battle with one another, the great beast turns his full attention on you, and you realize then that there can be no escape. You gulp in fear and try to force your brain into deciding what to do.

Fight to the finish! Turn to page 100 . . .
Curl up into a ball! Turn to page 105 . . .

You don't know exactly how you managed to get between the prince of demons and an aspiring set of his worshippers, but you don't see how sticking around to argue about it could possibly do you any good. You grab Yuk Yuk and Spiderbait by their hands and sprint for the back part of the cavern you're in, letting Ploopploopeen and Bloppblippodd battle it out for the fate of Sloobludop.

You discover that you're not the only one who's had that idea. Dozens of kuo-toa are running in the same direction as you. Being more comfortable in the water than on land, they don't move fast, and you and the goblins quickly outdistance them.

Once you reach the part of the cavern farthest from the Darklake's shore, you spot a passageway framed by blazing torches. The guard post there has been abandoned, so there's no one to stop you as you grab one of the torches and race into the darkness beyond.

Soon, Yuk Yuk asks to stop, pointing out that there's no way a creature the massive size of Demogorgon could follow you into a corridor this small, but you force the goblins to press on.

"It's a strange and wild world," you tell them, "and I wouldn't be surprised at all to run into a demon prince who could change his size at will."

"Do you really think he can do that?" Spiderbait asks.

"I have no idea," you reply. "And I have no desire to find out."

You keep moving until both of the goblins are so tired

that they can't make their legs go anymore. You reluctantly agree to a short rest, and you spend the entire time with your ears pricked, listening as hard as you can for any sign that the demon prince or any of his followers might be after you.

Turn to page 102 . . .

You might die today, but you're not going down without a fight!

"Come on, boys!" you say to Yuk Yuk and Spiderbait, who are still cowering under the Deep Father's altar. "Let's make this a death they'll tell stories about!"

Yuk Yuk cringes at the sight of your outstretched hand, but after considering it for a moment, Spiderbait reaches over and lets you haul him up.

He turns around and beckons to his brother. "Come on," he says to Yuk Yuk. "We had a good run, didn't we? Least we can do before that big monster kills us all is spit in his eye."

Yuk Yuk emerges from beneath the altar, wiping his runny nose with the back of his arm. He gives you a hard look, then turns to his brother. "I told you we should have left the human back on the Silken Path."

"Too late for that now." Spiderbait glances over your shoulder as Demogorgon lays into the first rank of the half-submerged towers that rise out of the shores of the Darklake. "Too late for anything."

The towers go down before the demon prince's might. The first one he strikes topples over and crashes into the one next to it. They both tumble in a loud and chaotic mess that splashes everything close by with brackish mud. For a moment, you hold your breath, hoping that the buildings might have somehow landed on the demon and crushed him, but you see his glowing faces emerge from the billowing destruction. His skull-splitting screech informs everyone in the cavern that he is still very much alive. And furious.

Bloppblippodd and her stalwart warriors march forth to greet Demogorgon. "All hail the Deep Father!" she shouts. "His faithful servants shall be rewarded!"

Demogorgon emerges from the destruction on the water's edge and stares down at Bloppblippodd and her warriors. This creature doesn't care about their misguided passions for him. All he desires is wanton destruction.

He swings his massive tentacles and sweeps away an entire row of kuo-toan warriors with a single blow. Their bodies splash into the waters of the Darklake, which greedily swallows them.

"No!" Bloppblippodd says as she recoils from the demon prince's wrath. "We called you here! We want to serve you!"

Turn to page 113 . . .

Eventually, you realize that if Demogorgon were really after you, by this point you'd already be dead. Knowing that the demon prince is down here in the Underdark, though, makes you even more determined to find your way to the surface.

Over the next several days, you push the goblins hard. You survive on water dripping into little pools here and there, and on mushrooms you find that the goblins declare safe to eat. Every time you come to a fork in the passages, you work your way farther and farther up.

One day you reach a large cavern, and something feels different. As you cross to the other side, you realize that you can actually feel a breeze coming from up ahead. And it carries the scent of fresh air!

"We made it, boys!" you tell Yuk Yuk and Spiderbait. "We're free!"

"You're free, you mean," Yuk Yuk says.

Spiderbait gives you a crushing hug. "Just do one thing for us. Don't forget us!"

Say good-bye. Turn to page 118...

Insist that they come with you. Turn to page 121...

Keeping your eyes on the ground, you answer the demon prince's question by shouting, "All hail Demogorgon, undisputed prince of demons!" Gesturing toward the kuo-toan you've skewered to the altar, you add, "Please accept my humble offering and spare my worthless life!"

The gigantic demon chuckles at your words. "Such boldness from such a lowly creature," his left head rumbles. "It offers us that entertainment, at least."

"But does it give us its loyalty?" the right head asks. "It's one thing to bring us the corpse of a fish man, but we have all of those we could ever need. What about its heart?"

"Shall we pluck that from its chest to find out?" the left head says. "It seems like such a waste."

Demogorgon leans down and lifts your chin up with its scaly, clawed tentacle until you are looking into its faces.

"Pledge your eternal loyalty to us," the demon prince says, "and we will consider your offer."

Never! Turn to page 116...

Hail, Demogorgon! Turn to page 110...

You stare up at Demogorgon, and the horror of the vision takes your mind and snaps it in half. His tremendous height. His backward knees. His scaly skin. His twinned baboon heads, which seem to be arguing with each other at every step, even to the point of snapping at each other with their vicious fangs.

It's all too much. You can't take it anymore. Not even for one more second.

You turn to look for the goblins and realize they're still hiding under Bloppblippodd's foul Shrine to the Deep Father. You fall to your knees and scramble under there to hide with them, but as you do, you know there's nowhere to hide.

"Are you okay?" Spiderbait asks.

You open your mouth, but you can't bring yourself to reply. You want to tell him no, you're not okay. None of you are okay. Nothing will be okay for any of you ever again.

"We're all going to die," Yuk Yuk says.

You reach out and cling to the goblin as some means of agreeing with him, and he's shaking like a leaf in a hurricane. It's a moment before you realize that it's you who's shivering, far, far worse than he is.

You hear the noise of utter destruction and screams of horror coming from the direction of the Darklake's shore. As you sit there, curled up in a ball with the two goblins clinging to you, the sounds come closer and closer. You know there's no escaping your fate, and you are too stunned to bring yourself to care.

Then the ground beneath you shakes with the tread of tremendous clawed feet, and you shudder so hard that you wonder how you haven't entirely fallen apart. There's a pause, and then the disgusting altar you've been hiding under disappears as Demogorgon plucks it up and casts it aside like a child's toy.

You stare up at the demon prince in staggering horror, and your mind goes blank. There's nothing left of you to

terrify because you've gone entirely away.

The gigantic demon leans over you with both of its faces and lets loose a screech of hellish harmonies that shatters your eardrums. You gaze up at him, your lips quivering.

And then you begin to laugh.

At first, it's just a gentle giggle, a tentative titter, but when the demon doesn't slaughter you for it, it grows. Soon you're chuckling, then outright laughing. Within seconds, you, and both of the goblins still clinging to you, throw back your heads and indulge in some unbridled cackling.

Demogorgon stares down at you for a long while. Eventually, one of the heads begins to laugh as well. The other head shakes back and forth in disgust. Then the demon prince strolls away, looking for other havoc to wreak.

Your mind is shattered. For years afterward, the denizens of the Darklake claim to hear your cackles echoing throughout the caverns and beyond.

THE END

You don't see any good way out of this. If you stand and fight Demogorgon, he's sure to kill you along with everyone else. But can you possibly outrun such a creature? If he wants to slaughter you, there's nothing you can do about it.

But maybe you can make it so he doesn't want to kill you after all. . . .

As the demon prince cuts his way through the worshippers that rush to greet him, you grab hold of the spear you thrust through the kuo-toan who died on the altar at your hand. Is that what finally brought the beast forth from the depths of the Darklake? Or were Bloppblippodd's entreaties always going to draw him here?

You have no way of knowing, but you're ready to stake everything on the off chance that the demon might have some shred of gratitude toward you. Even if he's not showing any to Bloppblippodd and her warriors right now.

You shush the goblins, who are still curled up beneath the altar, clinging to each other and shivering in fear.

"Whatever you do, don't make a sound," you tell them. "No matter what you hear me say or do. If we're lucky,

Demogorgon might not even notice you—but if you make too much noise, he will!"

The goblins fall silent then, and you hear not a word of protest from them. You watch as Ploopploopeen leads his warriors against the demon prince, knowing none of them have a chance. Part of you wants to leap forward and join the battle, but you know the only thing that will bring you is a quick and painful death.

Once Demogorgon finishes off all of the kuo-toan warriors in Sloobludop, he turns his fearsome attention to you. As he approaches the altar, you leap atop it and fall on your knees, head bowed, still holding tight to your spear.

The demon prince snickers once, and one of his heads says, "What madness is this?"

Turn to page 103...

You stare Demogorgon straight in both of his fiery faces and say, "Who would be so foolish as to lie to the demon prince of lies? I would not flatter myself to think I might be able to deceive the Great Deceiver. Not even for a moment!"

"Ha," the head on the left says. "Speaking of flattery, it will get you nowhere. Do you really think we're that stupid?"

The head on the right says, "Wait a minute. Give him the chance to speak."

The left head turns to the right and scowls at it in disbelief. "You do this every time," it says. "You let these mortals lie to you, and then you lap it up like you're starving for attention."

The right head arches an indignant eyebrow at the other. "And you never give anyone the benefit of the doubt. You think I don't know when someone's lying to us?"

"You think *I* don't? In this case, it's obvious!"

"Of course he's lying to us. What does that matter? I think you'd appreciate watching someone besides us do some lying once in a while. Why can't you ever just sit back and appreciate a decent lie for once? Is crushing this fool immediately so important that you can't manage to toy with him for a bit for our own amusement? You've grown so cold."

"I have not!" the left head smacks the other with his tentacle. "Shut up!"

"That's enough!" the right head says as it brings the nearest tentacle up and wraps it around the other's throat. "I've had it with you! You've finally crossed the line! It won't be tolerated any longer!"

The two tentacles begin thrashing at the two heads, and you step back, stunned at your luck. You edge away quietly from Demogorgon, beckoning to Yuk Yuk and Spiderbait to follow.

Turn to page 119...

Demogorgon strikes. More of Bloppblippodd's warriors fall before him, their blood staining the streets red.

Bloppblippodd turns and runs from the rampant destruction, straight to her father. She falls on her knees before him, weeping in terror. He reaches down to comfort her and orders his followers forward.

Plooploopeen's warriors—those hearty few who haven't already fled—rush forward to attack Demogorgon. While they are better prepared than Bloppblippodd's fools, they fare no better before the demon prince's power. He lashes out at them with unrestrained violence, and they fall like halfling children before an angry storm giant.

You scoop up a trident that one of Plooploopeen's warriors dropped as he fled. The goblins find spears that are too long for them to handle properly but seem to revive their flagging confidence.

"Wait for your chance," Spiderbait says to his brother.

"I won't miss," Yuk Yuk says as he plants the blunt end of his spear against Bloppblippodd's foul altar.

You can't save them. You can't even save yourself. But you're going to leave Demogorgon with a scar he'll remember forever.

THE END

Soon after, you emerge from the Underdark and find yourself on the side of a grassy hill that rolls down toward the endless sea. You stand there and bask in the warmth of the sun, breathing in the glorious fresh air. You take a moment to enjoy an incredible sense of triumph. Not only did you get free from those drow slavers, but you also made it back to the surface alive!

You walk to the west until you come across a road, which you decide to follow to the south. Soon you come upon the gates of the city of Waterdeep, and you cannot believe your luck. You had hoped to someday make your way here, but you never dreamed you'd reach it by such a twisting route.

As you enter the city, you stare up at the buildings in wonder. This is a place you could call home.

While you're standing there, a well-dressed man with a neatly trimmed beard approaches and says, "Hello, stranger! If you don't mind me saying so, you look lost!"

You smile at the man. "I don't know if I've ever been more found in my life."

"Ah, so you're a citizen of Waterdeep? My apologies."

"Oh, no," you say. "I've never been here before."

"I thought I recognized that look of wonder in your eyes!" the man says. "Might I interest you in one of my guidebooks, then? I wrote them myself!"

You stare at the handsome book the man hands you to peruse. The title on the cover reads *Volo's Guide to Waterdeep*. As you flick through the pages you realize just how much you may be in need of such an extensive guide. Maybe it could help to keep you out of such trouble in the future.

"Sorry, but I don't have any way to pay you at the moment," you confess.

Volo claps you on the back. "Not an unusual situation for those who can make the best use of my guides, I'm afraid. But you look like you need a favor and perhaps a friend. Read it and make good use of it. Then, once you're ready, pay me whatever you can."

"You'd loan me one of your books?"

"I don't think of it as a loan. I have a good eye for adventurers, and when it comes to you, I see this book as more of an investment."

A tingle of excitement rushes down your back and although you had thought that perhaps after recent events you were done with adventuring, you can't help but wonder what new escapade may be just around the corner.

THE END

You're just fine with lying to a demon, but when it comes to pledging your eternal loyalty to one, you find you just can't do it. You open your mouth to say yes, but the words stick in your throat. Instead, you stare up at the creature in terror and simply shake your head.

"I thought not," the left head says. "You're a brave fool to try to lie to the Lord of Lies."

"But bravery isn't what we want in our followers," the right head says. "We need obedience. And if we can't have that, we'll settle for outright madness."

Demogorgon's arms snake out and wrap you in his cold, slimy tentacles, wrenching the spear from your hand. You struggle to escape, but the demon prince only tightens his grip on you. You try to scream for the goblins to run, but you find you can't draw enough breath to make that happen.

Demogorgon lifts you up and raises you to his left head and then his right. Each examines you in turn, and you feel as if they can see into separate aspects of your soul.

You screw up your mouth and do the one thing you can still manage. You spit in the right head's eye.

As Demogorgon wipes your spittle from his right face, the left one starts to laugh. It's a horrible, bitter, vicious sound that seeps through your ears into your brain. You find that you can't help but laugh along with it, despite the fact that you don't find anything about this remotely funny.

"That's fine," the right head says while the left one keeps laughing. "We don't need you to pledge your loyalty to us. We'll take it anyhow."

At that moment, your mind goes blank, and you find that you no longer have the desire to escape, to harm Demogorgon, or to do anything at all. The only thing you know is that his laughter will ring forever in your ears, and that you will do whatever he desires as long as it does.

THE END

You kneel down next to the two goblin boys and give them a long hug. "I can't tell you how grateful I am to you both," you say. "Without the two of you I would surely never have made it out of that web, let alone back to the surface alive."

"We're going to miss you too," Yuk Yuk says. He starts to choke up a bit, but Spiderbait socks him on the arm.

"Just think of the stories we'll have to tell all the others!" Spiderbait says. "Two little goblins like us? Making friends with a human? And running up against Demogorgon?"

Yuk Yuk frowns. "No one's ever going to believe us."

"It doesn't matter what anyone else believes," you tell them. "You both know the truth. But I for one will spread the tale of how two goblins saved a lost human and faced one of the most terrifying things to haunt the Underdark."

With that, they give you one last hug good-bye. You turn and start toward the exit from the cave. As you get closer, you turn back to see the goblins one last time, but they're already gone.

Turn to page 114 . . .

You race to the back of the cavern as Demogorgon battles with himself. To your surprise you find Plooploopeen there, trying to sneak away from the fight too.

"Well done," he says to you. "I thought for sure we were finished."

"Which way to the surface?" you ask him.

Plooploopeen stands there for a moment as Demogorgon continues to tear his town apart. "I'll take you there myself. There's nothing for me here now."

Then the kuo-toan charges into the darkness with Spiderbait, Yuk Yuk, and you on his tail. You escape the demon lord's wrath and continue up, up, up. Days later, you finally near the surface, and Plooploopeen points you toward a shaft of sunlight blazing down from above.

"Go," he says, putting his hands on the goblins' shoulders. "I'll take care of these small fry."

The goblins give you a group hug and send you on your way—to sunshine and freedom!

THE END

A re you kidding?" you say to the two goblins. "I can't leave you here. Without you two, I never would have escaped the Underdark at all. From now on, the three of us stick together."

"But we're goblins," Yuk Yuk says in despair. "They won't let us into the cities we've heard about up there — places like Waterdeep and Neverwinter, or Baldur's Gate or even little Daggerford."

"They'll think we're evil," Spiderbait says. "They'll try to kill us on the spot. We're much safer down here!"

You kneel next to the two goblins and put your hands on their shoulders so you can look them straight in the eyes.

"I'm not going to lie to you," you tell them. "We've been through far too much together for that. You're right. If you come with me, I can't take you into any of the amazing cities along the Sword Coast. They won't trust you, even if I tell them about all the amazing things you've done for me."

The goblins' faces fall, and you realize they were hoping you knew of a place that would accept them the same way it would accept you. But you don't know of such a place. Not in the Underdark and certainly not in the world above it.

"But that's okay," you tell the goblins. "It's a big, wide, wonderful world out there, filled with sunshine and warmth and fresh air and fields you can run all day in and not find the other side. There's more than enough room for us there, outside of those cities. And plenty of adventure to be had as well, I bet."

You stand up and reach out your hands to the goblins. "It's your choice," you tell them. "I won't make you come with me if you want to return to the Underdark, but I would do everything in my power to ensure your safety above ground if you did want to join your paths with mine. What do you say?"

They glance at each other for a moment and then leap forward at the same time. You turn and lead them toward the incoming wind and the open lands beyond. Toward the light.

THE END

The images in this book were created by Adam Paquette, Aleksi Briclot, Bryan Syme, Claudio Pozas, Conceptopolis, Craig J. Spearing, Cynthia Sheppard, David Hueso, E. W. Hekaton, Franz Vohwinkel, Hector Ortiz, Ilich Henriquez, Jared Blando, Jasper Sandner, Jedd Chevrier, Kieran Yanner, Lars Grant-West, Olga Drebas, Richard Whitters, Sam Burley, Scott M. Fischer, Wayne England, and Zoltan Boros.

The cover illustrations were created by Eric Belisle, Ilich Henriquez, and Olga Drebas.

CANDLEWICK
ENTERTAINMENT

Copyright © 2018 by Wizards of the Coast LLC
Written by Matt Forbeck
Designed by Crazy Monkey Creative and Rosie Bellwood
Edited by Kirsty Walters
Published in the U.K. 2018 by Studio Press,
part of the Bonnier Publishing Group.
All rights reserved.

First U.S. edition 2018
Library of Congress Catalog Card Number pending
ISBN 978-1-5362-0242-7 (hardcover) 978-1-5362-0065-2 (paperback)
18 19 20 21 22 23 WKT 10 9 8 7 6 5 4 3 2 1
Printed in Shenzhen, Guangdong, China
Candlewick Press, 99 Dover Street, Somerville, Massachusetts 02144
visit us at www.candlewick.com

Don't miss the other Dungeons & Dragons® Endless Quest® titles!

Into the Jungle
To Catch a Thief
Big Trouble

Or these Dungeons & Dragons titles available from Candlewick Press:

Monsters and Heroes of the Realms
Dungeonology

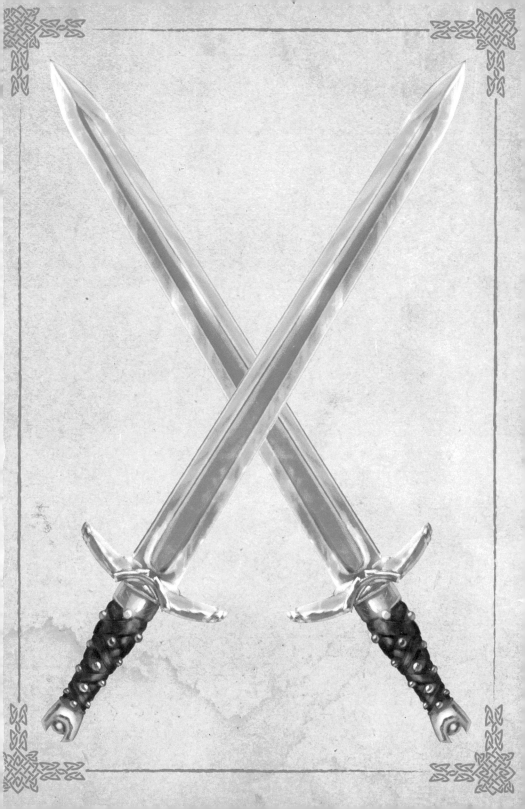